S M A R T
START MAKING A READER TODAY®

READERS CHANGE HISTORY

SMART presents this book to honor and recognize the
exceptional contributions of time, talent and friendship

ALICIA CHON

has given in her important volunteer service to,
and support of, the SMART Program at

BEAVER ACRES

as **SMART Site Coordinator 2008-2009**

Through her commitment to SMART she enhances and
energizes the program while positively impacting
young children's lives in extraordinary ways.

THANK YOU FOR ALL YOU DO, ALWAYS!

lauren child

I am TOO absolutely small for school

CANDLEWICK PRESS

CAMBRIDGE, MASSACHUSETTS

for Sofie and her
invisible friend
Søren Lorensen

and for Maisie, Clemmie,
Molly and Ella

No part of this book may be reproduced or stored in an information retrieval system in any form or by any means, graphics, electronic, or mechanical, including photocopying, taping, and recordings, or without prior written permission from the publisher. First U.S. edition 2004. Library of Congress Catalog Card Number 2003065576. ISBN 0-7636-2403-9. First published in Great Britain in 2003 by Orchard Books, London. Printed in China. This book was typeset in Officina Serif Book and Badloc. Candlewick Press, 2067 Massachusetts Avenue, Cambridge, Massachusetts 02140. visit us at www.candlewick.com The illustrations were done in mixed media.

10 9 8 7 6 5 4

I have this little sister, Lola. She is small and very funny.

Mom and Dad say she is nearly almost big enough to go to school.

Lola is not so sure.

Charlie

huge

giantish

big

biggish

smallish

slightly small

small

tiny

teeny

eeny weeny

Lola

says,

"I am **absolutely** not **BIG**.

I am still

really quite small."

Charlie

She says, "I probably do not have time to go to school. I am too extremely busy doing important things at home."

I say,
"At school
you will learn
numbers and how to
count up to one hundred."

Lola says,
"I don't need to
learn up to one hundred.
I already know up to ten
and that is plenty.

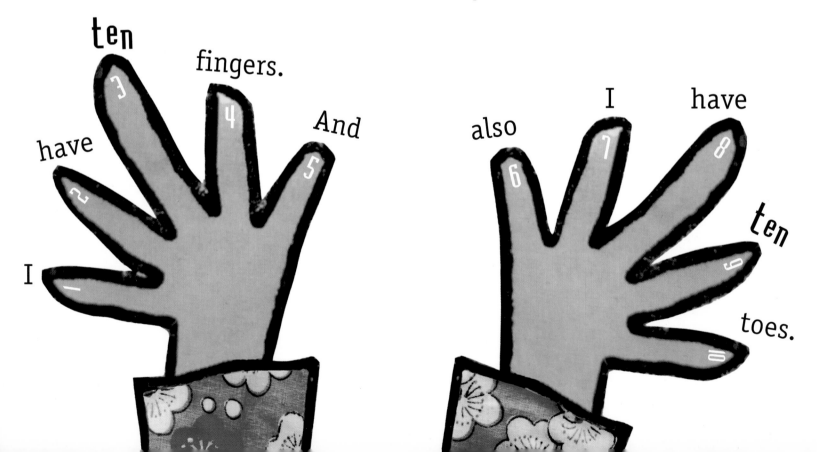

I have ten fingers. And I also have ten toes.

And I

Never

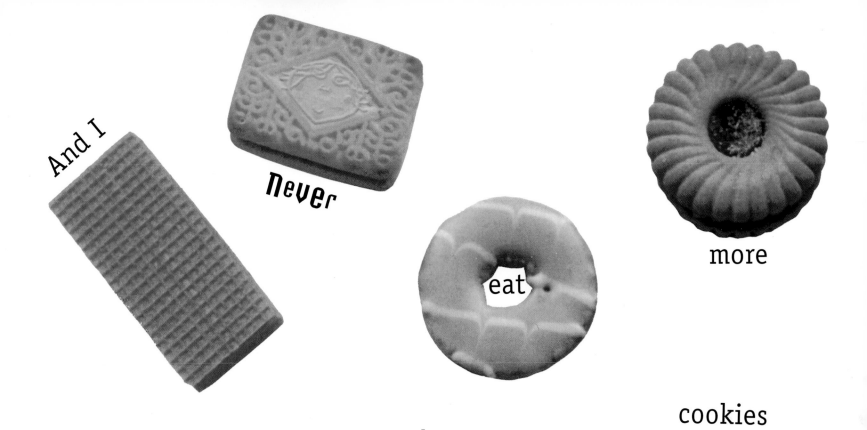

eat

more

cookies

than

ten

time.

at

One

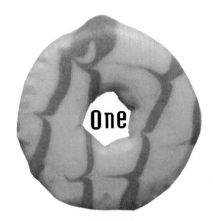

Ten is enough."

"But Lola," I say, "what if eleven eager elephants all wanted a treat.

I say,
"And what about learning your
letters, Lola?
If you know how to write,
you can send cards to
people you like."

"But not everyone has a telephone, you know,
Lola," I say.

"Who doesn't?" says Lola.

"Santa Claus," I say. "You have to write him a special note and send it to the North Pole to tell the

"Santa Claus," I say. "You have to write him a special note and send it to the North Pole to tell the

"And Lola," I say,
     "don't you want to
read words? Then you will
     be able to **read** your
own **books.** And understand
secret messages written
on the fridge."

     Lola says,
     "I know lots of **secrets.**
I don't need to **read words,**
          and I've got all my
books in my head.
     If I can't remember, I
can just make them up."

"But Lola," I say, "what would you do if there was an *ever so angry ogre* who would not go to sleep unless you read him his favorite bedtime story?"

Then Lola says,

"I **would** like to **read** to an ogre and **count up** elephants and send **notes** to the North Pole. But I **absolutely** will NOT ever wear a **schooliform**. I do not like wearing the **same** as other people."

I say,

"But Lola, you won't have to wear a school uniform. At our school you can wear **whatever you like**."

"**Oh**," says Lola.

"You wait there. I know **exactly** what I can wear. . . ."

"Well, Lola," I say, "that's certainly stylish,

but you **cannot** go to school dressed as a **crocodile**."

Lola says, "This is **not** a **crocodile**. This is **a alligator**."

I say, "You can't really go as **an alligator**, either."

"Why not?" says Lola.

My sister Lola is fussy about food.

"I like to wear **stripes**," says Lola, "but what will I do at **lunchtime**? You know I will **never** NOT EVER eat a **school lunch**."

I say, "But Lola, you can take your very own **packed lunch** in your very own **lunch box**."

Lola says,
"I do not want to eat at school,
alone, all by myself
on my own."

I say, "But Lola, at school you will meet lots of new **friends**. You can have **lunch** with one of them."

Then Lola says, "But I already have **my friend**, Soren Lorensen. I like to have **lunch** at **home** with him."

Soren Lorensen is Lola's invisible friend. No one knows what he looks like.

Walking to school, Lola is all wobbly.

She says, "Soren Lorensen is feeling slightly not very well."

He is worried he will not be able to count numbers, do letters and read words, and no one will

"Lola," I say, "it will be okay. You'll be fine. I bet you'll both have a really good time. And after school we'll have pink milk at home."

"talk to him, so he will be all by himself, on his own."

When school gets out, she's not by her peg.

But then there she is, and she's not all alone by herself, she's hopping along home with somebody else. . . .

At home, I say,
   "Lola, I **told you** that you would
        have a **good time**."
And Lola says,
   "Oh I know, Charlie, I was not
worried. It was Soren Lorensen
        who was nervous, **not me**.
        I was **fine**."